# Beetle and the Hamster

WITHDRAWN
FROM
STOCK

# Beetle and Friends

**Get together with Beetle
and his friends!**

Be sure to read:
 *Beetle and the Bear*

... and lots, lots more!

# Beetle and the Hamster

## Hilary McKay
### illustrated by Lesley Harker

■SCHOLASTIC

*For Emma Hipkin with love – H.M.*

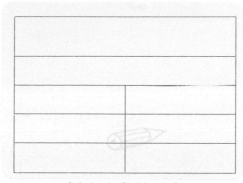

Scholastic Children's Books,
Commonwealth House, 1-19 New Oxford Street,
London, WC1A 1NU, UK
a division of Scholastic Ltd
London ~ New York ~ Toronto ~ Sydney ~ Auckland
Mexico City ~ New Delhi ~ Hong Kong

First published by Scholastic Ltd, 2002

ISBN 0 439 99445 4

Printed and bound by Oriental Press, Dubai, UAE

10 9 8 7 6 5 4 3 2 1

# ✏ Chapter One ✏

One day, during a boring maths lesson, Beetle's friend Henry said to Beetle, "How did you get your hamster, Beetle?"

It was something Henry had wanted to know for a long time. He had a hamster of his own, and he remembered very well how hard it had been to persuade his mother to buy it.

It had taken weeks and weeks of pestering. He had had to promise to be good for the rest of his life before she gave in.

It had been quite different for Beetle. Beetle's hamster had just appeared, with no fuss at all. Henry could not understand it.

He poked Beetle with his elbow, and asked again, "Beetle, how did you get your hamster?"

Beetle gave up pretending he was too interested in maths to notice Henry and said, "I can't tell you that."

"Why?" said Henry. "Have you forgotten?"

"No," said Beetle, "of course I haven't forgotten! I just can't tell you."

"Oh," said Henry, not very pleased, and then after a bit he said, "I thought you were supposed to be my friend!"

"I am your friend," said Beetle.

"Well, I didn't think friends had secrets. Not best friends anyway," said Henry. "I only wanted to know how you got your hamster!"

"Ask me anything else in the world, Henry," said Beetle kindly. "Ask me anything else in the world, and I'll tell you that instead."

Beetle leaned back in his chair and folded his hands behind his head and stretched out his legs. He was all ready to tell Henry anything in the world except how he got his hamster, but he did not get a chance.

Mrs Holiday, the class teacher, interrupted them. She often interrupted people's conversations.

"What is so interesting, Beetle and Henry?" she asked, in such a loud voice that Henry went bright red and Beetle tumbled off his chair with shock.

"I only asked Beetle how he got his hamster," said Henry. "But he says he can't tell me."

"Of course he can't tell you," said Mrs Holiday. "This is Maths, not Hamsters!"

"That's not why I can't tell you, Henry," said Beetle, picking himself up off the floor and sitting back down on his chair. "I can't tell you because I said I wouldn't. I promised I wouldn't tell anyone."

Not far away sat a girl called Lulu. Beetle carefully did not look at Lulu, and Lulu carefully did not look at Beetle.

They were the only people in the world who knew how Beetle had got his hamster.

# Chapter Two

It had happened like this.

Beetle had been out in his garden digging.
He was trying to find a worm. Beetle
wanted a pet very much and he thought
a worm might do.

Lulu, who lived next door, had climbed up her side of the fence and was hanging there watching him. She was gnawing the top of the fence as she watched. It had got quite wet.

Lulu was planning something, Beetle could tell. He wondered what it was, and why she was gazing at him so thoughtfully.

"Are you coming over?" he asked.

Lulu shook her head. "You might as well get down then," said Beetle.

Lulu smiled and shook her head again.

"Oh, well," said Beetle, and he gave up trying to get rid of Lulu and carried on with his digging as if she was not there. But she was there. And she was the kind of girl it was hard not to look at. Even when she was chewing a fence.

After a while Lulu said,
"I think I'll have you
for my boyfriend!"

"What!" said Beetle.

"I'm having you for my boyfriend," said
Lulu calmly. "All the girls in our class have
boyfriends. I might as well
have you. You're
the nearest.
You will do."

Beetle was stunned. Could she choose him
just like that? Didn't he get to decide too?

"So," said Lulu, speaking through a mouthful of fence, "prove you're my boyfriend! What will you give me if I kiss you?"

"Kiss me?" repeated Beetle in amazement. "What will I give you if you *kiss me*? Are you crazy? I only came out here to dig for worms!"

"I never said you couldn't dig," said Lulu,
still chewing the fence. "I said, *What...*"

But Beetle did not wait to hear any more.
He picked up his spade and went to dig
behind the shed where
Lulu could not see him.

# Chapter Three

Behind the shed was not a good place for worm digging. The ground was too hard and Beetle's father's oily old bike kept getting in the way. Beetle gave up after a while and sat down and thought about things instead. He thought about Lulu and he thought about pets. Then he thought about Lulu's pets.

Lulu had loads of pets.

"Too many," said Lulu's mother, who had to look after them all.

Lulu had rabbits, goldfish,

a guinea pig, and two budgies.

She even had a tortoise, but the pet that Beetle liked best was the hamster. He had taken care of it once, when Lulu went on holiday.

"It bites," she had warned, but it had not bitten Beetle. He had got very fond of that hamster.

He had hated having to give it back when Lulu finally remembered to come round and collect it.

Beetle shuffled uncomfortably.

He wanted to come out from behind the
shed but Lulu was still hanging on the
fence. She was humming
now, humming and
gnawing together.
She paused to call,
"Beeeeetle! What
will you give me if..."

Then Beetle had a sudden and terrible idea, and before he could think about it he had done it. He rushed out from behind the shed and shouted, "What will you give me if *I* kiss *you*?"

Lulu was so surprised that she slipped backwards off the fence and disappeared.

She didn't stay down for long though. She scrambled up again almost at once, and asked, "What do you want?"

"The hamster," said Beetle.

That surprised Lulu even more.

"Is that all?"

"Yes," said Beetle.

"Then you'll be my boyfriend?"

"If I get the hamster."

"Promise?"

"Promise."

"All right."

"All right," said Beetle.

Lulu shut her eyes and offered him a cheek and waited.

Nothing happened.

"Go on then," she ordered after a moment. "Do it."

"Get the hamster first," said Beetle.

# Chapter Four

To Beetle's surprise Lulu did as she was told. She hurried away at once. A minute later she was back again, and Beetle saw with a thumping heart that she was carrying the hamster's little cage.

She passed it over the fence to him and then climbed across herself.

"Remember it's not yours till you've kissed me!" she told Beetle. "And then you'll have to be my boyfriend! Don't forget! A promise is a promise!"

Beetle took no notice. He was too busy opening the door at the top of the cage to lift the hamster out.

"You be careful!" warned Lulu. "It's still my hamster!"

It was a very fast hamster. In one second it was out of the cage,

across Beetle's hand,

and racing over the grass, making straight for the worst place in the garden.

The worst place in the garden was the compost heap. It was made of soggy leaves and vegetable peelings, old tea bags, banana skins, black grass and slugs.

The hamster seemed to love compost. It raced up and down and round and round and in and out of tunnels and caves.

"Get my hamster out of there!" squealed Lulu. "Quick!"

Beetle dived into the compost heap. It was like diving into an enormous smelly pudding.

The hamster seemed very happy exploring the compost pudding. It always managed to keep just in front of Beetle's grabbing hands.

And for some reason the compost did not seem to stick to the hamster. It kept perfectly clean. Beetle did not.

"Help me!" he shouted to Lulu, but Lulu would not help. She was laughing so much she could hardly stand up.

She wobbled around laughing and holding her nose and reminding Beetle that it was still her hamster, but she would not come and help catch it.

Then the hamster got tired of the compost
heap and made a dash for the dark space
under the shed.

Lulu stopped laughing and shouted,
"Get it! Get it!
It's still my
hamster!"

# Chapter Five

The space under the shed was the second
worst place in the garden. It was very
narrow. Beetle had always thought it was
too small to crawl under, although just
the right height for snakes and spiders.
He lay down on his stomach and peered
into the darkness.

It was musty and cobwebby there. He had to look for a long time before he spotted the hamster. It was curled into a small golden ball, right in the middle, too far away to reach.

"I think it's asleep!" he whispered to Lulu.

"Catch it before it wakes up then!"

Beetle took a deep breath and pushed further under the shed. Dust filled his eyes and nose and soft things flapped against his bare neck.

He could only move by pushing himself along using his elbows and his toes. It seemed a very long time to Beetle before his fingers finally closed around the sleeping hamster at last.

"Got it!" he called to Lulu, who was peering under the shed.

"It's still my hamster! Bring it to me quick! Hurry!" said Lulu.

"How can I hurry, stuck under this shed?" muttered Beetle.

"What?"

"Nothing," said Beetle.

He looked around for the easiest way out.
Moving backwards was too difficult, so he
carried on forwards.

After what seemed like hours there was
open space in front of his face. He gave a
final push with his toes, and at last came
out into the lovely
sunlight.

Then just when he thought he was free, he
bumped into his dad's oily old bike and it
fell down flat on his head.

"OOOOWWWWW!" moaned Beetle,
rolling and groaning with his head clutched
in one hand and the hamster in the other.

Lulu ran round the back of the shed to see
what all the moaning and clattering and
banging was about. When
she saw Beetle she said,
"Yuk! Beetle!
You look awful!
Give me back
my hamster!
I've changed
my mind!"

# ✏ Chapter Six ✏

Beetle struggled out from under the bike.
He was black with dust and compost. Blood
from a long scratch trickled down one arm.
There was a slug in his hair, cobwebs
hanging down his neck, and bike oil
smeared all over his face.

"I've definitely changed my mind!" said Lulu. "Give me back the hamster! I'm definitely not having you for a boyfriend!"

Beetle wiped a dirty hand across his hot, oily forehead, tipped the hamster gently back into his cage, and said, "A promise is a promise. I've got to kiss you and you've got to give me the hamster."

"I think you should have a bath," said Lulu, picking up the hamster cage.

"A bath?"

"Or a shower. Or a bath and a shower," said Lulu, walking backwards very fast. "And all clean clothes, and a bandage on your arm..."

Lulu was walking and talking at the same time and by now she had reached the fence.

She began to climb. She was escaping.

Suddenly Beetle knew that if he didn't do something fast he would have no hamster after all his trouble.

That was why
he kissed Lulu.

On the back of one elbow as she was
scrabbling over the fence. She nearly made
it, but she didn't.

When she found she
had not escaped
Lulu turned back
around and
grabbed Beetle
by the hair.

"All right," she said. "But promise you will never tell anyone how you got the hamster!"

"I promise," said Beetle.

"Never?"

"Never," said Beetle.

"A promise is a promise. But perhaps we could share him. Perhaps he could be your hamster and visit me sometimes."

"No," said Lulu. "He can be your hamster, and visit me sometimes. A promise is a promise."

That was why Beetle would not tell Henry how he got his hamster. Even though he was quite happy to tell him anything else in the world. Because, as he and Lulu completely agreed, a promise is a promise.

These days Beetle and Lulu found they agreed about quite a lot of things, and Beetle had given up trying not to look at Lulu. It was easier to look.

Henry thought Lulu was very pretty too. He often went round to Beetle's house so that they could all three meet at the end of the garden to chew the fence, and admire each other's teeth marks, and talk about everything in the world. Except hamsters.